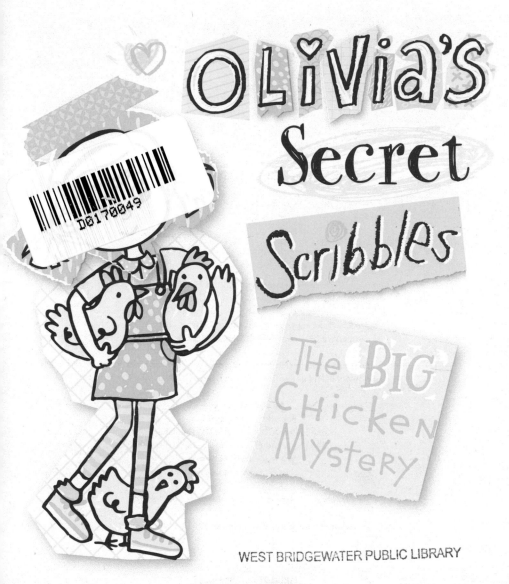

OLIVIA'S Secret Scribbles

The BIG Chicken Mystery

Kane Miller
A DIVISION OF EDC PUBLISHING

With thanks to Abbie, Annabelle, Bailey, Camilla, Lexie, Molly and Robyn Donoghue from Tucker Road Bentleigh PS and the Duck Pond Duckies for their egg-cellent ideas!—M.C.

For my fellow chicken lovers, Ray, Jade and Zoe.—D.M.

First American Edition 2021
Kane Miller, A Division of EDC Publishing

Text copyright © Meredith Costain, 2019
Illustrations copyright © Danielle McDonald, 2019

First published by Scholastic Australia Pty Limited in 2019.
This edition published under license from Scholastic Australia Pty Limited.

Library of Congress Control Number: 2020949880

Printed and bound in the United States of America

1 2 3 4 5 6 7 8 9 10

ISBN: 978-1-68464-301-1

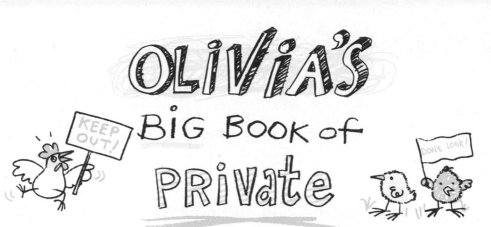

OLIVIA'S BIG BOOK of PRIVATE

SECRETS

DO NOT OPEN!

GO AWAY!

(This means you, Ella!
And you too, Max!!)

Hatch Day Monday

Today was the best school day ever!

Our chickens had their first hatch day!
A hatch day is like a birthday, except it's for
chickens instead of people. It celebrates
the day they hatched out of their shells!

Today the chickens turned one year old!
We had a big party for them in their
chicken run.

Mr. Platt made special cakes for them out
of watermelon, lettuce, yogurt and corn.
Chickens ♥ watermelon. And so do I. ☺

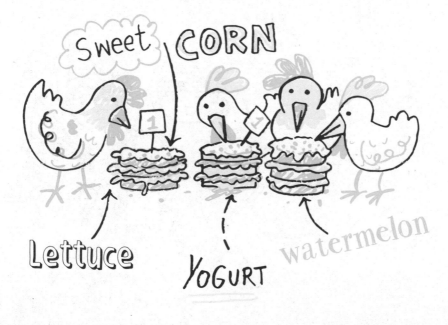

Sweet CORN

Lettuce

YOGURT

watermelon

Then we all played chicken games with them. Harry and Ava showed us how to do a special chicken dance!

I can't believe we have
had these chickens
now for a whole year! I
remember when they
started out as eggs in a

glass box in the corner of our classroom.
One day, the chicks inside started to peck
away at their shells until . . .

They hatched! Then they
huddled under a heat
lamp to keep warm.

At first the chicks were all wet and floppy. But then they turned into sweet little fluff balls!

FLUFF BALLS!

The baby chicks were so cute! They stumbled around on their little legs, bumping into each other.

The chicks stayed in a big box in our classroom for six more weeks!

We weighed them,

we measured them,

and we cuddled them.

Then we gave them all names:

Bella

ROXY

JUMBO

Henny-PENNY

Tara

PeaRLie

Dixie

BETTY

Sweetie

Summer

Jumbo, Dixie, and Betty turned out to be roosters! So we had to give them away to a farm.

When they were big enough, we moved the chicks into a brand-new chicken coop near the bike shed at school. They have lots more room to walk around in there. And we can visit them whenever we want!

Our chickens are all grown up now. We take turns to feed them and collect their eggs. Sometimes we even read them stories.

My favorite chicken is Pearlie. When she was a baby hatchling she followed me around everywhere. I think she thought I was her mom.

She still comes when I call her now.

After the hatch—day party we went back
to our classroom and wrote stories about
the chickens. Mine was all about Pearlie
being a pirate!

--PiRate
PearLie

Mr. Platt read some of our stories out
loud. Everyone loved my pirate story! Then
he said he is going to be making a special
announcement tomorrow.

YESSSS!

I ♥ special announcements. They always mean something really awesome is going to happen.

I wonder what this one will be?

A ROLLER-SkaTing contest

A PET eLepHant

A school trip to the MOON

I can't wait to find out!

livia

Special Announcement Tuesday

Mr. Platt told us his special announcement first thing in the morning. And it was about Mrs. Burkin. Mrs. Burkin was our teacher last year.

Mrs. Burkin's new class has been hatching chicks, just like we did. And now their chicks are old enough to move to the big chicken coop. But there is only enough room in the chicken coop for one group of chickens at a time. And now that the new chicks are coming, we need to find new homes for our old chickens!

Mr. Platt asked if anyone would like to take some chickens home. But if anyone does, they have to take at least two. That's because chickens don't like being on their own. They like hanging out in big groups. Just like all the kids on my soccer team!

Everyone put their hand up straightaway!

My hand went up the highest. I want
Pearlie to live at my house! And Pearlie's
best friend, Roxy, so she doesn't get lonely.
We could have heaps of fun together!

I'm going to tell Mom and Dad all about it at dinner tonight. They are going to love Pearlie and Roxy as much as I do.

☺livia

After dinner . . .

At dinnertime, I told everyone about Pearlie and Roxy coming to live with us.

MOM

MAX

ME

ELLA

DaD

Me: Guess what?

Ella: You slipped on a banana peel.

Me: No, I didn't. I don't even like bananas.

Ella: Yes, you did. And you went for a ride.

Me: Did not.

Ella: Did.

Me: Mo—om. Ella's being mean again.

Mom: Ella. Stop being silly and eat your dinner. What did you want to tell us?

Me: Mrs. Burkin's class had baby chicks!

Dad: Did they really?

Me: Yes. And now they are old enough to move into the *big* chicken coop. And *our* darling chickens have to move out.

Mom: Oh. Poor chickens.

Then Mom and Dad explained why we couldn't keep Pearlie and Roxy here. There were so many reasons!

Reason Number 1:

Chickens are very messy. They would leave chicken poop everywhere.

Reason Number 2: Chickens need lots of looking after. Who was going to feed them? And check that they had water? And where would they live?

Reason Number 3:

They might eat all the plants in Dad's veggie garden.

Dad's Veggie Garden

Reason Number 4: What about Bob?

He might chase them!

Or they might chase him!

Reason Number 5:

Chickens are very noisy. They might annoy the neighbors.

It's so not fair. Pearlie and Roxy would never do any bad things like that. They are the best chickens in the world!

I need to find a way to show Mom and Dad that having chickens is a good thing! Then they'll let them come here for sure.

I'm going to start first thing tomorrow!

livia

Good News Wednesday

Matilda and I spent all lunchtime in the library, thinking up lots of good things about chickens. Matilda is my BFF. Her backyard is right behind ours! We do everything together.

Our librarian, Mr. Snarski, offered to help us. He loves chickens too. ☺

matilda

ME

MR. Snarski

Here is what we wrote.

WHY IT IS GOOD TO HAVE CHICKENS AT YOUR HOUSE

by Olivia and Matilda

1. Chickens lay eggs. Mostly every day! So you don't have to spend any money buying eggs at the store. You can just walk outside and there they are! Eggs are very healthy and good for you.

Ba-Gawwk!

You can eat them for breakfast.

Breakfast

Or make cakes with them.
And also pancakes. (Yum!)

← Pancakes

Or juggle them.

"BOING!

Boing!

Or do scientific
experiments with them.

2. Chickens ♥ eating bugs and snails. Which will be very good for Dad's veggie patch. Because his best veggies are always being eaten by bugs and snails and this makes him VERY cross.

But if the chickens eat the bugs and snails, Dad will stop being cross and will be SUPER HAPPY instead! He might even make us all pancakes as a special treat. ☺

3. Chicken poop is good for Dad's veggies too. It will help them to grow big and strong. And also tasty.

4. The chickens will eat all the vegetable peelings from when Mom or Dad cooks them for dinner which means we won't have to throw them away in the garbage. Which is very wasteful and bad for our planet.

5. They are fun to be around! (Not like big sisters who never let you play with them and their friends or let you in their room.)

6. Pearlie will miss me and be sad if she can't come here to live with us. And then I will be sad too. ☹

The End.

I showed our list to Mom and Dad as soon as I got home. They read all my points very slowly and seriously.

But I think Dad might have something wrong with his eye. It kept twitching while he was reading it.

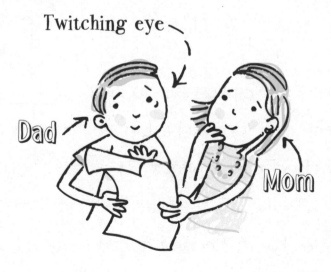

Twitching eye

Dad

Mom

And guess what?

They said yes!
Pearlie and Roxy
can come here
to live in our
backyard. Dad
even said he
will help me build a special
chicken coop for them!

But only if I promise to look
after them properly. I have to feed them.
And check their water. And collect their
eggs. Every day. (Matilda is going to help
me do this. I already asked her.)

And also clean up any mess they make. (This part will be easy peasy . . . I hope.)

Cleaning up mess

I'm so happy! I can't wait to tell Mr. Platt.

And Pearlie and Roxy!

☺livia

Big Problem Thursday

Now I have a new big problem.

Lots of other kids in our class want to
take chickens home too! And they all have
really good reasons. ☹

I will play with them every night as well. And also teach them how to do karate.

Hiyah!

NiCO

Our backyard is really big. It's perfect for chickens.

sage

Our backyard is even bigger. So it's even more perfect.

Samira

Our backyard is ginormous. It even has a moat!

BetHany

I think Bethany made this bit up.

But there aren't enough chickens for everyone to take some home. So Mr. Platt is going to run a competition. We have to design our perfect chicken coop.

And the best three coop designs win a prize!

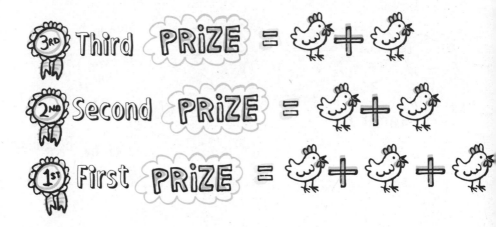

This is going to be easy peasy for me. I am super awesome at drawing and designing things.

I already have lots of plans for amazing inventions and machines up here in my bedroom.

Ideas

Here are my top three.

Supersonic thrusters

MY SPACE ROCKET

1. My space rocket with supersonic thrusters that can take you all the way to the other side of the galaxy. (And also back again.)

2. My homework-doing and bed-making robot. (With a built-in snack maker.)

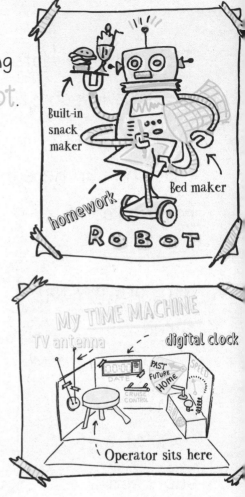

Built-in snack maker

Bed maker

homework

ROBOT

3. My time machine.

This one is nearly finished.

My TIME MACHINE

TV antenna

digital clock

DATE

PAST FUTURE HOME

SPEED

CRUISE CONTROL

Operator sits here

I'm going to win one of those prizes for sure! ☺ ☺ ☺

livia

After dinner . . .

Here are some of my designs for the
Perfect Chicken Coop competition.
I really, REALLY hope I win. Then
Pearlie and Roxy
can come and
live at our
house forever!

Space coop

SKYLIGHt

EGG
SLIDE

Nesting
pods

Egg catcher

Ramp

Coop on wheels

hanging plant

Fairy LIGHtS

Nesting boxes

WHeeLS

Deluxe coop

Swimming Pool

Rooftop garden

STRICTLY NO FOXES ALLOWED KEEP OUT!

Edible plants

I'm going to enter the Deluxe Coop design because it is the best one ever!

I hope Mr. Platt thinks so too. ☺

livia

Fabulous Friday

Guess who won the chicken coop
competition? It was . . .

And because I came first, this means
three beautiful chickens are coming to live
at our house instead of two. (Oops!)

I don't think Mom is very
happy about the extra
chicken. ☹

But Dad is. Especially when I told him this means there will now be lots more chicken poop to put on his veggie garden.

And also lots more eggs to make pancakes. ☺

Harry's and Bethany's chicken coops won second and third prize. So they are getting chickens too. This is who we all chose.

Me:

PeaRLie   ROXY

Sweetie

Harry:

Henny-PENNY Tara

Bethany:

Bella Summer

Matilda didn't win any chickens. But that's OK. She's going to share mine. ☺

Dad and I went to the store after school to get lots of hammers and nails and other building stuff. We're going to have a big working bee on the weekend.

A working bee is when lots of people come together to help make or fix something.

I don't know why it's called a working bee because there are no actual bees involved.

Our chicken coop is going to be supercool! I've had some brilliant ideas for some extra-special super-duper features that we can add to it.

Chicken Coop Features

Automatic food feeder

FOOD goes HERE.

Chicken PECKS food HERE

Automatic water-drinking machine

WATER falls DOWN into HERE

OLD bucket

CHICKEN DRINKS from HERE.

OLD BOWL

Chicken CLIMBING Ladder

Knobbly BRANCHES

♡ 44 ♡

Nesting boxes

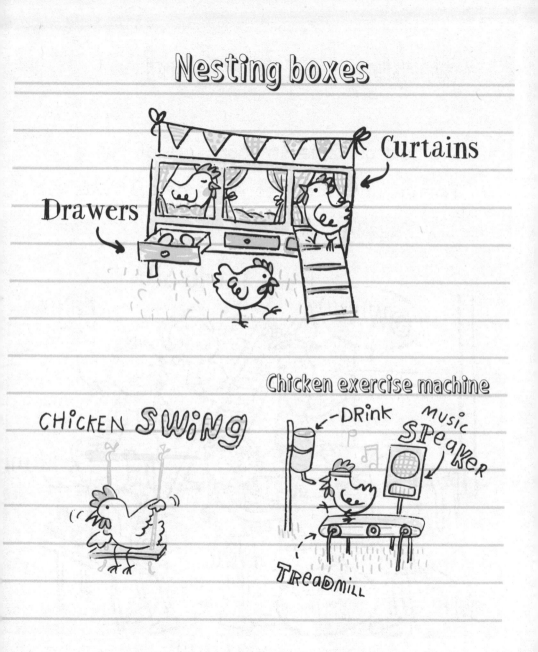

Curtains

Drawers

Chicken exercise machine

CHICKEN SWing

DRink

MUSIC SPEAKER

TREADMiLL

Working Bee Weekend

We built our chicken coop! Lots of our friends and family came to help. It was so much fun!

Ella and her BFF, Zoe, painted little chicken-and-egg designs on the walls.

ELLA

ZOE

And Max collected a whole bucket of snails from Dad's veggie garden, ready for the chickens to eat when they come home tomorrow.

Pearlie and Roxy and Sweetie are going to love it for sure.

 Olivia

Magic Monday

The chickens are here! ☺☺☺

I was hoping Dad would pick us up after school in a chicken mobile!

Chicken mobile

SIDE VIEW   FRONT VIEW

But it was just his car.

Mrs. Freeman, our next-door neighbor,
let us borrow her cat carrier to put
Pearlie and
her friends in.
I don't think
Donkey was
very happy
about that.

Donkey

Donkey lives next door with Mrs. Freeman.
His real name is Marmaduke. But he
and I both think Donkey is a much
better name!

I've been training Donkey to be a detective cat. But he's not very good yet. I think he's a little bit lazy. He loves lying in the sun on the roof outside my bedroom window. And sleeping on my bed.

I wonder if Donkey will like our chickens. Chickens ♥ being up high, just like he does. Maybe they can all hang out together!

Donkey

Chickens

Dad put some straw in the bottom of the carrier in case the chickens made a mess on the way home.

They did. 🙁

When we got home we made sure Bob was safely locked inside. We didn't want him chasing the chickens on their first day here. (Or the chickens chasing him!)

We put the carrier down on the lawn. Matilda opened up the little door. But the chickens all

Matilda

stayed inside, clucking softly. I called to Pearlie.

HERE, Pearlie. Here, chick, CHICK, chick!

Pearlie poked her head out of the carrier.

I called her again. Pearlie stepped out and looked around. Then she came running toward me, flapping her wings and squawking.

BUK, Buk, Buk!

I put *some* grain in my hand and she pecked it all up. Then she jumped up on my shoulder and pecked at my ear.

Hee hee!

PearLie

Roxy and Sweetie stepped out too. They pecked around our feet, looking for food.

I put Pearlie back down again. Then I sprinkled more grain on the ground in a long trail. Just like the one in Hansel and Gretel. It led all the way to the chicken coop.

The chickens followed my trail all the way
inside the gate. ☺

Then they made themselves nice and
comfy in their new home. I think
they're really going to like it.

livia

Trouble Tuesday

As soon as school finished, Matilda and I raced home to see our chickens.

How many eggs do you think our girls laid today?

Gazillions! We can have pancakes every day!

YAY!

We went straight around the back to our backyard. And guess what?

The chicken coop was empty. All the chickens had disappeared!

"Maybe they escaped," Matilda said.

We looked behind
all the plants

and under the outdoor
tables and chairs

and through the hole in the fence that
leads to Matilda's backyard,
and up in the tree.

But we *still* couldn't
find them.

Matilda pointed at something orange in the middle of Dad's veggie patch.

"What's that?" she asked.

"Bigtooth," I told her. "Max's favorite dinosaur. He must have dropped it there when he was looking for snails."

BIGTOOTH

I looked around for Bob. I couldn't see him either! Maybe they were all together somewhere? Making a big mess!

I ran inside to find Mom.

Matilda and I headed straight for Max's bedroom. Mom came too.

But guess what? The room was empty!

It smelled REALLY bad though.

MEOW!

Donkey walked into the room with his tail in the air. Then he disappeared under the bed!

Mom lifted up the bedspread.

Max and Bob and all the chickens were cuddled up together under the bed, watching a Superchicken movie.

Clever Donkey led us straight to the chickens. Maybe he is going to be a good detective cat after all! ☺

livia

No Eggs Wednesday

Matilda and I checked the chicken coop as soon as we got home from school today. This time, the chickens were all inside, clucking quietly. Phew.

I made sure there was food and water in their feeders. Then I looked inside the first nesting box. It was empty. So was the second nesting box. And the third one.

Our chickens hadn't laid any eggs!

EMPTY
Nesting boxes

They didn't lay any yesterday either.
Pearlie, Roxy, and Sweetie always laid an
egg every day at school.

Something must be wrong.

livia

Big Idea Thursday

We had a big chat with Bethany and
Harry about our chickens at school today.

Me: Our chickens haven't laid
any eggs yet.
Harry: Same. Not even one.
Bethany: Bella and Summer
haven't laid any either.
Matilda: Maybe they're bored.
Harry: Why would they be bored?
Me: I know! Because they're used to
seeing each other every day, like we do.
And now they can't.

Bethany: Yes! That's it! Poor little chickens.

Matilda: We need to do something that gets them all together again. Even for just a day.

That's when I had a brilliant idea.

Got to go. Mom's calling me for dinner. I'll tell you all about it when I come back!

livia

After dinner . . .

Here's my brilliant plan to help our bored
chickens. Bethany and Matilda both think
it's supercool!
We can have a . . .

Sleepover PARTY!

In our backyard!

I'm also going to ask Ella for some extra
ideas. She always has excellent sleepover
parties.

Here are the awesome things we can do.

SUPER-DUPER SLEEPOVER PARTY FOR BORED chickens!

1. Give all the chickens chicken manicures.
And paint their nails in pretty colors.

ME →

Pearlie ↓

Nail Polish

2. Make party hats for them!

3. Dress them up in sweet little outfits from Ella's Big Box of Dress-Up and have a chicken fashion parade.

4. Play party games, like Pin the Tail on the Chicken. Or Chicken Jump Rope!

5. Sing songs about chickens to them.

6. Make them yummy snacks.

FOOD GARLAND TREAT

CORN

7. Read them spooky stories about ghost chickens!

BOO!

BA-GAWWK!

Now all I have to do is ask Mom if we can have the Super-Duper Chicken Sleepover Party at our place tomorrow night.

I'm going to go downstairs and show her my plans for it right now.

Mom loves eating eggs for breakfast. She's going to say yes for sure!

livia

A bit later . . .

Mom said no.

☹☹☹

Big Fail Friday

Still no eggs.

Harry said Henny-Penny and Tara aren't laying any eggs either. Not even teensy tiny ones. And yesterday they got into big trouble.

Harry and his dad saw the chickens flying over the fence. They had to chase them down the street and bring them back again.

HARRY

BA-GAWWK!

Harry's DAD

Where were they going? 😟

Secret Garden Saturday

It was Nanna Kate's birthday today. (She's MUCH older than our chickens.) Mom and Dad took us all out to lunch to help her celebrate it.

Nanna Kate

The café we went to is called The Secret Garden. It's in a big community gardening place where people can grow their own veggies and flowers. Nanna Kate grows tomatoes and beans and sunflowers.

And sometimes broccoli. 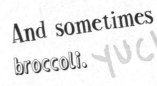YUCK

She told us the food in The Secret Garden café is really yummy. And guess what? It was! Even though it had vegetables in it. (Vegetables. Erk.)

Here is some of the food you could have:

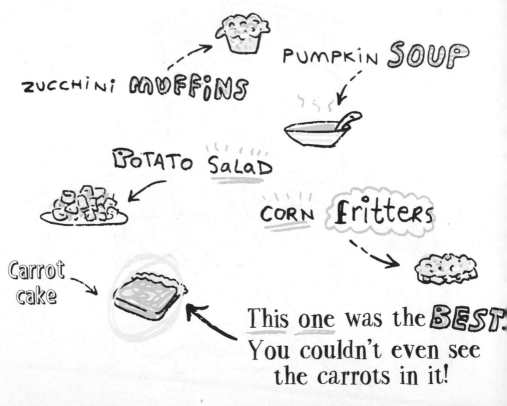

ZUCCHINI MUFFINS

PUMPKIN SOUP

POTATO SALAD

CORN fritters

Carrot cake

This one was the BEST. You couldn't even see the carrots in it!

And guess who we saw there?

Bethany!

Me: Hi, Bethany!
What are you doing
here?
Bethany: Helping
my mom. She runs
the café with my Aunt Tess.
Me: Cool. What's the bucket for?
Bethany: To get snails. Aunt Tess says
the veggie plots here are full of them!
Me: Dad's garden is too. Snails LOVE
veggies.

Bethany: I know.
But they're eating
all the veggies Mom
wants to use for the café food.

Me: What are you going to do with all the snails?

Bethany: Take them home for Bella and Summer. They LOVE snails.

Me: Our girls love snails too.
Hey, why don't I
go and get Max?
He loves looking for
snails. I bet we find
heaps.

Bethany: Cool! I'll get more buckets.

Max and I helped Bethany collect snails from all the different garden plots. Max found the most!

WOW! There are millions of them.

I asked Bethany if Bella and Summer had laid any eggs yet. But she said they hadn't.

I wonder why not?

It's a chicken mystery.

Olivia

Soaker Sunday

Something really bad happened last night.

I forgot to lock up our
chickens. And they all
escaped!

And guess where Pearlie and Roxy spent
the night?

On top of Mr. Pappas's clothesline.
Cuddled up together inside a pair of his
ginormous undies.

OOPS!

Mr. Pappas lives next door. He showed us a
photo he took of our naughty chickens
this morning.

I don't think he was very happy.

And guess where Sweetie was?

In Mrs. Freeman's pear tree. She gently coaxed Sweetie out with her water soaker.

WATER SOAKER

I don't think Mrs. Freeman is very happy either. She says our chickens make too much noise.

ALL DAY Long!
Cluck cluck cluck.
Cluck cluck cluck.

I wonder why the chickens flew out of our garden. The chicken coop we made for them is really nice and comfy.

Harry's chickens tried to escape as well.

Why? There has to be a reason. I just don't know what it is. The chicken mystery continues!

I'm going to have a big think and try to work it out.

livia

A bit later . . .

Mom and Matilda and I had a big talk all about the chickens.

Me: I used to think our chickens were bored.

But now I think it's something else.

Matilda: Me too.

Mom: What do you think now?

Me: I think they're all sad.

Mom: Why do you think they are sad?

Me: Because they all grew up together, ever since they were tiny little baby fluff balls.

Matilda: Yeah. And then they all got split up and sent to different homes.

Me: But if they could all live together again, they'd be happy, chirpy chickens.

Matilda: They might even start laying
eggs again!
Me: Mmmm. Pancakes. 😊
Matilda: And egg sandwiches!
Mom: And scrambled eggs for breakfast!

And then I had a . . .

BRiLLianT IDEA!

The most brilliant idea I've ever had! But
I'm going to be much too busy to tell you
about it now.

You'll just have to wait until later!

☺livia

Sunday, two weeks later

I haven't been writing things down lately.
I've been much too busy!

We've just come home from the
community garden. That's where our
chickens live now.

And guess what? Henny–Penny and Tara

live there now too. And so do Bella and Summer!

That was my BRiLLianT IDEA!

After our talk with Mom, Matilda and I decided we needed to find a way to bring all the chickens back together again.

Forever. So we had a big talk with Harry's parents and Bethany's mom.

Harry's mom said maybe the chickens kept trying to fly over the fence because they were looking for their friends.

And Bethany's mom said there are enough bugs and snails and vegetable peelings at the community garden and café to feed all our chickens for years.

And guess what? Everyone thought my idea was brilliant too!

YAY!

Our family and friends came back to my house for another working bee. They helped us to pull apart our chicken coop. Then we loaded all the bits onto the back of my Uncle Stu's truck and drove to the community garden.

Then we built a new Super-Duper DELUXE chicken coop, right outside the back door of The Secret Garden café!

SUPER-DUPER →
DELUXE chicken coop

I'm a bit sad that Pearlie and her friends don't live with me anymore. ☹ But I can visit them at the community garden any time I want. And Harry and Bethany can visit their chickens too. ☺☺☺

And guess what? Bethany's mom told us our chickens have been laying eggs all week. With beautiful golden yolks.

So now the café has a new menu . . .

Pavlova
with strawberries and cream

YUM!

Scrambled eggs

Cheese omelette

Spinach frittata

And they all taste YUMMY!

livia

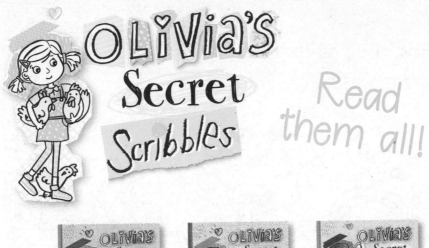

OLIVIA'S Secret Scribbles

Read them all!